Shapes in Transportation

Jennifer Rozines Roy and Gregory Roy

Marshall Cavendish
Benchmark
New York

We're going on a road trip to visit our friends who live in the city.

We'll take our car for transportation. Transportation is the way we get from one place to another.

We can look for shapes along the way. A shape can be made from straight lines or curved lines, or both.

Buckle up! Off we go!

We drive down the street then stop!

At the end of the street is a stop sign. A stop sign is a shape with eight sides. It is called an octagon.

The speed limit sign shows how fast we can drive. It is a rectangle. It has four sides and four right **angles**. An angle is made by two straight lines that meet in a point.

That traffic light ahead is also a rectangle. But there are even more shapes on it: red, yellow, and green circles! A circle is a curved, unbroken line with no angles.

Circles are very useful in transportation. Their shape helps you move over land smoothly, because they don't have corners, or angles.

If wheels were rectangles, it would be a bumpy ride!

Shapes that have straight lines or straight sides are called polygons. A polygon with three sides and three angles is called a triangle.

Up ahead is a "no passing zone." The sign for it is a triangle.

This sign is a triangle, too. It is turned, or rotated, in a different way than the first triangle sign.

Triangles can look different from each other, but they always have three sides.

To get to our friends' house, we need to drive over a bridge. This bridge has many triangles.

Sometimes two triangles together form a shape called a parallelogram. A parallelogram has four sides. The opposite sides are **parallel** and equal in length.

The whole bridge is the shape of a trapezoid. A trapezoid has four sides, but only two of the sides are parallel.

Squares have four sides, too. Unlike parallelograms and trapezoids, squares also have four right angles. All the sides of a square are the same length.

Diamond shapes also have four equal sides. But a diamond doesn't have right angles. A diamond is a **rhombus**.

When you turn a square, it may look like a diamond, but it is still a square.

Polygons can have even more sides and angles.

A school crossing sign has five sides. It is called a pentagon.

There is a school bus parked at the school. The bus wheels are circles, of course. But look closer and you'll see another shape. The lug nuts that hold the wheels onto the bus are shapes with six sides called hexagons.

Polygons come in all different shapes *and* sizes!

There's another octagon straight ahead. Stop!

Should we turn left or right at the stop sign? Or go straight? Let's check the map.

We are on Eleventh Street where it meets Seventh Avenue.

On the map, roads are straight or curved **line segments**. A line segment has a starting point and an ending point. The point where two line segments meet is where they intersect.

line segment —

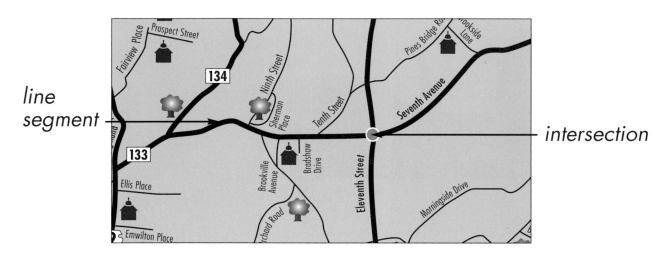

intersection

The point where two roads meet is called an intersection. That is where we are stopped right now. The map says we need to stay on Eleventh Street. So we'll drive straight through the intersection, past the point where the roads meet.

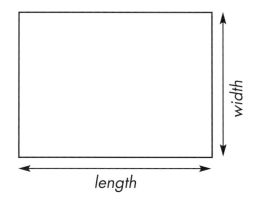

width

length

Our map is flat. Flat shapes are called two-dimensional. This is because they have only two **dimensions**: length and width, but no height.

But many things we see in our world are not flat. They take up space. That big truck driving next to us takes up a lot of space on the road!

The side of the truck is a rectangle shape. But the truck is not flat. It is shaped like a box, with six rectangular sides. A shape that takes up space is called a space figure. A space figure has three dimensions: length, width, and height. A space figure may be hollow or solid inside.

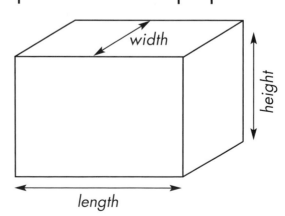

The truck is transporting letters and packages. Inside are hundreds of shapes: rectangles, solids with rectangular sides, and cubes.

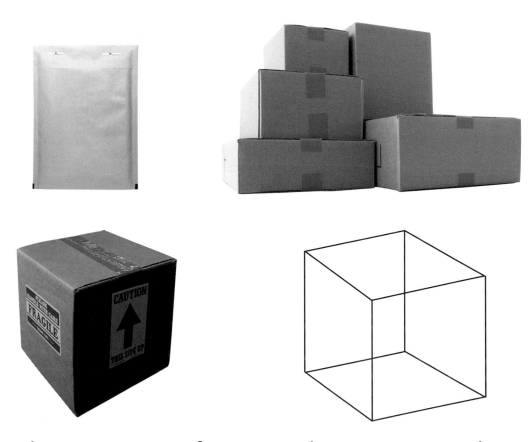

Cubes are space figures with six square sides that are the same size.

Airplanes will deliver these letters and boxes all around the globe. After all, Earth is a space figure, too. It is a sphere, or a ball shape!

Railroad crossing! The railroad crossing sign is shaped like an "X", with two intersecting rectangles. The gate is down, so we must stop and let the train pass.

While we wait, let's see what shapes go by.

That boxcar is made up of rectangles. It is a space figure called a **prism**. The tanker car has circles on each end and a curved surface. It is space figure called a **cylinder**.

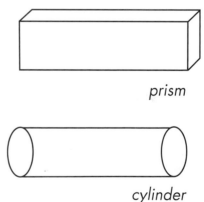

prism

cylinder

The train has zoomed by. The gate is up. We can drive over the railroad tracks and finish our journey.

Now we're entering the city. We see more space figures like the pyramid on top of that building. A pyramid is made up of triangles on a base.

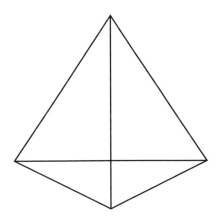

We pass a construction zone. They are fixing up the road for better transportation. The workers put orange traffic cones out to warn drivers to drive carefully around that area.

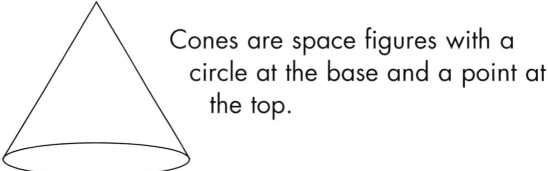

Cones are space figures with a circle at the base and a point at the top.

We drive past the construction zone then make a right. We're here! Our friends are waiting for us in that apartment building.

We made it in good time — and in good shape!

Glossary

angle — The shape formed by two straight lines that meet in a point.

cylinder — A hollow or solid shape with a curved surface and parallel circles of the same size on both ends.

dimension — A measurement of an object in length, width, or height.

line segment — A long, narrow mark with a starting point and ending point.

parallel — Lines that lie in the same direction and are always the same distance apart. Parallel lines never meet.

prism — A solid shape with sides that are parallelograms and ends that are equal and parallel.

rhombus — A flat shape that has four equal sides and, usually, no right angles.

Read More

Adler, David. *Shape Up!* Holiday House, 2000.

Murphy, Stuart. *Circus Shapes.* HarperTrophy, 1998.

Web Sites

Federal Highway Administration
http://mutcd.fhwa.dot.gov/signs/index.htm

PBS Kids Cyberchase
http://pbskids.org/cyberchase/games/23dgeometry/index.html

Street Signs U.S.A.
www.street-signs-usa.com

Transportation Wonderland
http://education.dot.gov/k5/gamk5.htm

Index

Page numbers in **boldface** are illustrations.

About the Authors

Jennifer Rozines Roy is the author of more than twenty books. A former Gifted and Talented teacher, she holds degrees in psychology and elementary education.

Gregory Roy is a civil engineer who has co-authored several books with his wife. The Roys live in upstate New York with their son Adam.

Marshall Cavendish Benchmark
99 White Plains Road
Tarrytown, New York 10591-9001
www.marshallcavendish.us

Library of Congress Cataloging-in-Publication Data

Roy, Jennifer Rozines, 1967–
Shapes in transportation / by Jennifer Rozines Roy and Gregory Roy.
p. cm. — (Math all around)
Summary: "Promotes recognition of shapes on the road, including street signs and bridges; stimulates critical thinking;
and provides an understanding of math in the real world"—Provided by publisher.
Includes bibliographical references and index.
ISBN-13: 978-0-7614-2265-5
ISBN-10: 0-7614-2265-X
1. Shapes—Juvenile literature. 2. Geometry—Juvenile literature. 3. Transportation—Juvenile literature.
I. Roy, Gregory. II. Title. III. Series: Roy, Jennifer Rozines, 1967– Math all around.
QA445.5.R69 2006
516'.15—dc22
2006010308

Photo Research by Anne Burns Images

Cover Photo by *SuperStock*/age fotostock

The photographs in this book are used with permission and through the courtesy of:
Corbis: pp. 1, 22 Aaron Horowitz; pp. 7, 13BL, 23L, 26 Royalty Free; pp. 8, 13BR Alan Schein; p. 20BL Bill Varie;
p. 20TR JPL/Deimos. *Woodfin Camp and Associates*: pp. 2, 4, 5, 9, 15R, 25 Chuck Nacke; pp. 6, 13TL Michael Heron;
p. 13TR Timothy Egan; p. 19 A. Ramey; p. 23R Dan Budnik; p. 24 Frank Fournier. *SuperStock*: pp. 10T&B, 11 Michael Gadomski;
p. 12B Mike Ford; p. 14 Creatas; pp. 15L, 18 age footstock. *Index Stock Imagery*: p. 12T Rudi Von Briel; p. 16 Tim Haske;
p. 20TL Image Source; p. 21 AbleStock.

Series design by Virginia Pope
Illustration page 7 by Augustus Boehling

Printed in Malaysia
1 3 5 6 4 2

My First Book of Buddhist Treasures

Illustrated by Peggy Walker

TREASURE
TOWER
BOOKS

Published by Treasure Tower Books
The children's book division of the SGI-USA
606 Wilshire Blvd.
Santa Monica, CA 90401

ISBN 978-0-915678-81-5

Cover and interior design by
SunDried Penguin Design

All quotes are excerpted with permission
from The Writings of Nichiren Daishonin, Vol.1
© 1999 Soka Gakkai

Printed in Korea

10 9 8 7

Library of Congress Cataloging-in-Publication Data

Walker, Peggy.
    My first book of Buddhist treasures / illustrated by Peggy Walker.
      p. cm.
Summary: A collection of short quotes from The Writings of Nichiren Daishonin,
accompanied by explanations and discussion questions, reveal the concepts and practices of
a particular form of Buddhism.
ISBN 0-915678-81-0 (Hardcover : alk. paper)
1. Nichiren,--1222-1282--Quotations--Juvenile literature.
2. Nichiren(Sect)--Doctrines--Juvenile literature.
[1. Nichiren,--1222-1282--Quotations.   2. Buddhism.   3. Spiritual life--Buddhism.] I. Title.
BQ8349.N577W25 2003
294.3'4432--dc22

2003022075

Contents

Teaching Others Like Nichiren Daishonin Did

"At first only Nichiren chanted Nam-myoho-renge-kyo, but then two, three, and a hundred followed, chanting and teaching others."

—The Writings of Nichiren Daishonin, p. 385

Daishonin means "great sage," a very wise person.

Buddha is a person who is very wise, kind, happy, full of hope, and helps others become the same.

Shakyamuni Buddha lived in India thousands of years ago. What he taught became known as Buddhism.

Each year on April 28 we celebrate the day when Nichiren Daishonin first taught about Nam-myoho-renge-kyo.

Who would you like to talk with about Nam-myoho-renge-kyo? When do you think it is important that we be brave and speak out?

Millions of people all around the world chant Nam-myoho-renge-kyo today. But 750 years ago, no one did. Nichiren Daishonin was the first person to teach people that they could become happy by chanting Nam-myoho-renge-kyo.

When Nichiren Daishonin was alive, people had forgotten what Shakyamuni Buddha had taught thousands of years before: that all people are equal and that everyone is a Buddha inside. He had to remind them, but not everyone believed him. Some people even thought he was lying, and they caused him lots of trouble. But he cared for the people so much, he bravely continued to teach them how to be happy.

We, too, can teach others about Nam-myoho-renge-kyo so that we and they can become happy. In this way, we can help bring peace to the world.

4

Nam-myoho-renge-kyo Is Inside Us

"Therefore, when you chant myoho *and recite* renge, *you must summon up deep faith that Myoho-renge-kyo is your life itself."*

—The Writings of Nichiren Daishonin, p. 3

A prayer is a deep wish or hope. When we pray, we chant Nam-myoho-renge-kyo, thinking about what we want. Through our chanting, as we get stronger inside, our prayers will be answered.

Life force means the energy and power we have inside. When our life force is strong, things go our way and we are healthier and happier.

What good things are inside you? How can you bring them out?

Nam-myoho-renge-kyo is another name for the Buddha. We all have Nam-myoho-renge-kyo in us. That means we are all Buddhas, filled with good fortune, a strong life force, wisdom, courage, kindness and many more good things. When you chant, you wake up the Nam-myoho-renge-kyo in your life and bring out all those good things. You become stronger so that you can solve all your problems, get answers to all your prayers, and help all your friends become happy, too.

When you have a hard time or feel scared, you might forget you are a Buddha. That's the time to chant and believe that, every time you look in a mirror, a Buddha is looking back at you.

The Gohonzon

"I, Nichiren, have inscribed my life in sumi ink, so believe in the Gohonzon with your whole heart."

—The Writings of Nichiren Daishonin, p. 412

Go means "worthy of honor," and *honzon* means "object of devotion."

Waking up our Buddhahood means becoming the strongest, healthiest and happiest that we can be on the inside.

In what ways can you be a better friend? A better student? If the Gohonzon is inside everyone, how do you think we should treat everyone?

Nichiren Daishonin wrote the Gohonzon. Down the middle, he put "Nam-myoho-renge-kyo, Nichiren." This shows that his life and the life of the Buddha or the life of the universe are all one. Can you imagine? The whole universe is on the Gohonzon. Your life, too, is one with the whole universe. One wise man called the Gohonzon a "happiness-manufacturing machine." Because the Gohonzon is so special, we take good care of it in our altars.

The Gohonzon, or Buddha, is inside each of us, too, so we should also take good care of ourselves. By chanting to the Gohonzon on the outside, we wake up our Buddhahood on the inside. That's how we can become stronger and wiser and be a better friend and a better student and a better whatever-we-want-to-be.

Prayers Are Powerful

"Muster your faith, and pray to this Gohonzon. Then what is there that cannot be achieved?"
—The Writings of Nichiren Daishonin, p. 412

W e can pray, or chant, for anything we want. Our prayers can be for something like "no more war" or playing your best in sports or doing your best on a test at school or helping a friend feel better. When you chant, you can accomplish whatever you want.

Just like your body needs food every day, your life needs Nam-myoho-renge-kyo every day to stay full of energy. Your toys work better when their batteries are charged. Chanting, even for five minutes a day, is like charging the batteries of your life. When you chant Nam-myoho-renge-kyo every day, you will be full of energy and good fortune. Keeping your batteries charged will help you to be happy and healthy all throughout your life.

This quote is from a letter that Nichiren Daishonin wrote to a girl named Kyo'o and her parents, Shijo Kingo and Nichigen-nyo. Kyo'o was only one year old at the time. Shijo Kingo was one of Nichiren Daishonin's most trusted followers.

Good fortune means the good things that happen to you.

When do you chant? What are some of the things you chant for? How long do you like to chant every day?

Never Give Up

"The journey from Kamakura to Kyoto takes twelve days. If you travel for eleven but stop with only one day remaining, how can you admire the moon over the capital?"
—The Writings of Nichiren Daishonin, p. 1027

Whatever we want to do, it's important to not give up. Sometimes when we try to do something, like learn about math or shoot a basket or play the piano, we might not do very well at first. That might make us feel angry or sad or even make us want to give up. But if we keep trying, no matter what, we will someday be able to do it.

Sometimes our prayers don't come true right away. It's like when you plant a seed; the flower needs more than a day to bloom. But so long as you decide to never give up and always chant Nam-myoho-renge-kyo, your prayers will all surely be answered.

Kyoto was the capital of Japan in 1280 when Nichiren Daishonin wrote this letter. Back then, people had to walk or ride horses or carriages, so traveling the two hundred miles between Kamakura and Kyoto took twelve days!

Who do you know who never gives up? What have you decided to do, no matter what? If you chant for something and it doesn't happen right away, what do you think you should do?

12

Cause and Effect

"Just as flowers open up and bear fruit, just as the moon appears and invariably grows full, just as a lamp becomes brighter when oil is added, and just as plants and trees flourish with rain, so will human beings never fail to prosper when they make good causes."

—The Writings of Nichiren Daishonin, p. 1013

Every time we make a cause, we get an effect. When we make good causes, we get good effects. When we make bad causes, we get bad effects. If you hit someone or say mean things (a bad cause), that person may hit you back or not like you anymore (a bad effect). But when you help a friend or study hard and listen to your teacher (a good cause), you will get a good effect, like a hug or a good grade (a good effect).

Chanting Nam-myoho-renge-kyo is the best cause we can make. It brings out the best in us and helps make everything we do have the best effects.

A cause is something we do, something we say, or something we think.

An effect is something that happens to us.

What kind of cause do you think is good? What kind is bad? If someone hits you or says mean things to you (a bad cause), what can you do that would be good causes to make things better?

Let's Get Benefits

"If you believe in this sutra, all your desires will be fulfilled in both the present and the future."

—The Writings of Nichiren Daishonin, p. 750

We chant to make our dreams come true and to become the happiest people we can be. We call this getting benefits. Some benefits you can see easily, like when you get a new pet or the bully at school stops bothering you.

But the best benefits are harder to see. They are the happiness, wisdom and courage that grow inside you every day, just like an acorn growing little by little until years later it's a big oak tree. Keep chanting every day, even a little bit, and you will one day grow to be like a big tree of happiness.

A *sutra* is a book that contains a Buddha's teachings. "This sutra" means the Lotus Sutra, which teaches that every person is a Buddha. We read part of this sutra every day when we do our prayers.

What are some of the benefits you've gotten? What are some benefits you want to chant for? Tell about the kind you can see and the kind you cannot see.

16

Our Buddhahood Protects Us Always

"Like a lantern in the dark, like a strong guide and porter on a treacherous mountain path, the Gohonzon will guard and protect you, Nichinyo, wherever you go."
—The Writings of Nichiren Daishonin, p. 832

The universe is full of many natural forces that support and protect us. When we really want something and make good causes to get it, these universal forces help us. But it's up to us to take the first step.

These forces come in all different forms. Sometimes they are people we know—friends, parents, teachers, neighbors, brothers or sisters. Sometimes they are animals or nature or other things around us.

Wherever they come from, all these forces get stronger as our lives become stronger inside. The more you chant, the more powerful your life becomes, like a strong magnet, pulling help and protection from everything around you.

Universal forces are sometimes called "Buddhist gods." The names of some Buddhist gods, like Sun and Moon, are written on the Gohonzon.

Nichinyo was a follower of Nichiren Daishonin in Japan. There is little information about her, but we know that the Daishonin wrote two letters to her, and it appears that she had very strong faith.

In what ways do these natural forces—these Buddhist gods— help you?

Offerings Say "Thank You"

"Whether you chant the Buddha's name, recite the sutra, or merely offer flowers and incense, all your virtuous acts will implant benefits and roots of goodness in your life."
—The Writings of Nichiren Daishonin, p. 4

A boy named Virtue Victorious wanted to give an offering to Shakyamuni Buddha. He had nothing to give except a pie made of mud. Because his offering came from his heart, in his next life he was born as a great king called Ashoka.

What's your favorite way to say thank you to the Gohonzon?

When we really want to thank people or show them that we love them, we often give them a gift. Sometimes we write them a note or give them a present or just spend some time with them.

In the same way, we can give gifts—no matter how small—to show our thanks to the Gohonzon. These gifts are called offerings. An offering could be ringing the bell or washing a piece of fruit for the altar. Sometimes our offering can be our time and effort, like when we go to a Buddhist meeting or chant with a friend.

What matters most is to make offerings because we really want to. Remember that, because the Gohonzon is inside us, we're really saying thank you to ourselves.

Changing Bad Into Good

"Just as poisonous compounds are changed into medicine, so these five characters of Myoho-renge-kyo change evil into good."

—The Writings of Nichiren Daishonin, p. 1064

"Five characters" refers to the Japanese way of writing. Some Japanese writing uses symbols, called characters, instead of letters. It takes five of these characters to write "Myoho-renge-kyo."

妙
法
蓮
華
經

How have you or your parents changed poison into medicine? Are there any bad things happening to you now that you want to change into good?

Sometimes bad things happen, like when you fight with a friend or fall off your bike. You might feel sad. Or you might be afraid to ride your bike again. When you really want to, though, you can turn anything bad that happens to you into something that can help you become happier. That's how much power you have inside you.

Even though you may be sad or scared or even mad, try to chant. When you do, remind yourself that you will be happy, no matter what. When you decide to turn poison (something bad) into medicine (something good), just see what happens! The friend you had a fight with can become your best friend ever, or you can learn to be the best bike rider in the neighborhood. It's all up to you.

The Mighty Lion's Roar

"Nam-myoho-renge-kyo is like the roar of a lion. What sickness can therefore be an obstacle?"
—The Writings of Nichiren Daishonin, p. 412

The lion is sometimes called the "king of beasts." When he roars, all the other animals pay attention. When we chant Nam-myoho-renge-kyo, we are like the lion king, and the whole universe pays attention.

Obstacles are things that try to keep us from becoming happy. But nothing can stop us when we chant. When you get sick or have a hard time learning to read or to add and subtract, don't be sad. Remember you are the lion king and you have the roar of the lion king, Nam-myoho-renge-kyo. Just keep chanting and keep trying and you'll win over all your obstacles.

Some obstacles, or problems, come from outside us, like germs that make us sick. And sometimes obstacles come from inside, like when we lose hope or think we are bad. Chanting Nam-myoho-renge-kyo helps us to overcome both kinds.

What problems do you have now? How do they make you feel? How do you think chanting can help you?

Always Have Hope

"Although I and my disciples may encounter various difficulties, if we do not harbor doubts in our hearts, we will as a matter of course attain Buddhahood."

—The Writings of Nichiren Daishonin, p. 283

Everyone has doubts or times when we are unsure about something. Nichiren Daishonin teaches us not to hold on to doubts. Ask questions, find answers, and chant until you don't doubt anymore. This way, doubts can help you be happier and more positive.

What was the hardest thing you ever learned to do? How did you do it? What ways can you help someone else who is having a hard time?

Even when we chant, we sometimes will have problems. Not understanding your homework or getting sick or fighting with your best friend can upset you. You might even feel that you will never be happy. But Nichiren Daishonin tells us to never doubt that you will overcome all your problems and become happy.

Doubt means that you don't believe you can do something. The first time you tried to roller skate, maybe you fell down and got hurt a little bit. But you just knew you could skate, so you kept trying and now you can! Or maybe you studied hard and now you understand your math homework. No matter what happens, always have hope that things will be better, because they will be. Chanting Nam-myoho-renge-kyo helps us solve all our problems.

26

Death Is Part of Life

"According to the Buddha's golden words, in the next life you are certain to be reborn in the pure land of Eagle Peak. What remarkable rewards you will gain!"
—The Writings of Nichiren Daishonin, p. 1097

Eagle Peak is a mountain in India where Shakyamuni often spoke. The top looks like an eagle's head and many eagles live there. When Nichiren Daishonin writes "the pure land of Eagle Peak," he means Buddhahood.

What can you do to feel better when you're sad? Why do you think chanting for someone who has died makes you feel better?

Have you had a pet that died? Do you know a friend or relative who has died? It can be very sad because we miss them. Sometimes we feel better when we understand that, even after death, their life is still all around us in the universe. Life lasts forever.

Being alive is like when we're awake during the day, and dying is like going to sleep at night, when we rest and prepare for the next day. After death, our lives are sleeping and getting ready to wake up into new lives.

Because chanting reaches everywhere in the universe, we can chant for those who have died. Our prayers comfort and help protect them while they "sleep" and help them to be reborn more quickly. By chanting throughout our lives, we can have a peaceful sleep at the end of this life and awake rested and happy in our next life.

Putting Fear in Its Place

"Each of you should summon up the courage of a lion king and never succumb to threats from anyone. The lion king fears no other beast, nor do its cubs."

—The Writings of Nichiren Daishonin, p. 997

Everyone gets scared sometimes. But deep inside us we are brave like lions. When we are brave, we can stand up to anything. We might still be scared, but being brave means doing what's right, whether we are scared or not. Every time we are afraid to do something but we do it anyway, we grow stronger. We learn that we don't need to be afraid of anything. Chanting Nam-myoho-renge-kyo helps us to become brave like lion kings.

Succumb means to give up or give in.

Nichiren Daishonin was very brave and never gave in to those people who wanted him to change his beliefs.

What are you afraid of? What do you think your parents are afraid of? How do you feel when you face your fears after chanting about them?

You Can Make a Difference

"If the minds of living beings are impure, their land is also impure, but if their minds are pure, so is their land. There are not two lands, pure or impure in themselves. The difference lies solely in the good or evil of our minds."

—The Writings of Nichiren Daishonin, p. 4

Ow we see the world around us depends on how we think and feel inside. When you're happy and smiling, people usually smile back. When you yell and scream, people get angry. When you're happy, even a rainy day is great. When you're sad, even a sunny day feels bad to you. Our minds—how we think and feel—determine everything. The good news is that we can control our minds. It's all up to us, and chanting will help.

You and your environment are connected. That's why when you change how you think and feel, you can change the world around you. The more hopeful, positive, wise and kind you are, the more the world around you becomes a great place to live. Even changing big things, like stopping pollution, starts with "cleaning up" how you think and feel.

Environment means everything that surrounds us— our homes, our families, our friends, the trees, the sky.

What things can you do to make a difference in your home? In your neighborhood? At your school?

32

Caring About Others

"To the Buddha, all living beings are his children."

—The Writings of Nichiren Daishonin, p. 535

Everyone in the world is part of the same big human family. No matter what we look like or where we come from, we all deserve to be happy. But when people in our family are unhappy, it's hard to be happy ourselves. When we help them to be happy, we feel happier, too.

One of the best ways to help others be happy is to chant Nam-myoho-renge-kyo for them, praying for their happiness, even for those who are mean to us.

We can also help others by telling them about Nam-myoho-renge-kyo. This starts a wave of happiness that spreads from one person to another—all over the world.

One reason we chant is to bring peace to the entire world. By becoming happy ourselves and sharing Buddhism with others, we create peace in the world every day.

Other children at school or even your brother or sister can sometimes be mean. What do you think would happen if you chanted for their happiness? Why do you think it is important to do so?

34

Thanking and Respecting Others

"Ever since I . . . undertook the practice of the Buddhist teachings, I have believed it is most important to understand one's obligations to others, and made it my first duty to repay such debts of kindness."

—The Writings of Nichiren Daishonin, p. 122

Lots of people help us every day. Our parents love and protect us. Our teachers teach us. Our friends play with us. Other people we don't even see help us, too, like the person who makes the clothes we wear, or the farmer who grows the food we eat.

Sometimes people who give us trouble also help us. For example, if a friend hurts your feelings, you might decide to chant to understand your friend's feelings. Chanting in this way will help you become a more caring person who tries to understand others—even those who are having a bad day or who sometimes do something mean.

One of the most beautiful ways to behave is to show respect to everyone and everything that help us. Remember that every person is a Buddha on the inside. Thanking all the Buddhas in your life will bring you lots of happiness and good fortune.

Obligation is something we have promised to do, no matter what.

How many people can you think of to whom you can show your thanks? How would you like to thank them? What reasons can you think of to feel thankful for someone who gives you a hard time?

Good Friends

"If we have even enough wisdom to distinguish hot from cold, we should seek out a good friend."

—The Writings of Nichiren Daishonin, p. 598

Distinguish means to tell the difference between one thing and another.

In Buddhism, a *good friend* means someone who helps others chant Nam-myoho-renge-kyo and practice Buddhism correctly so they can solve their problems and become happy.

How do you think you can be a good friend to someone? What can you do when one of your friends is sad or scared? What can you do if one of your friends does something you know is wrong?

A good friend is more than just someone you like or someone you have fun playing with. A good friend makes you feel better when you're sad or says "You can do it!" when you're trying something hard. Good friends are brave enough to remind you not to do things that could hurt you or others, like smoking or bullying someone.

When you have a fight with a friend, it's time to learn: did you hurt that friend? If so, you can learn to say you're sorry. Did your friend do something to hurt you? If so, you can learn to forgive. It's just as important to be a good friend as it is to have a good friend. Good friends are the treasures of life.

Cape Cod is a popular location for sailing.

From her, Joanne learned the importance of supporting herself with her own career.

Joanne attended private schools in Boston. During her summers, she spent hours sailing in the waters off Cape Cod. This sparked her curiosity about weather and clouds.

As a teenager, Joanne still loved flying. She even worked at Boston Airport. When she was 16, Joanne earned her private pilot's license. Like sailing, flying fueled her interest in clouds.

WOMEN'S WORK

Joanne finished high school in 1940. Then, she began college at the University of Chicago in Illinois. There, she decided to take a **meteorology** course.

Joanne enjoyed learning about weather. She decided to focus on this field. She met with Professor Carl-Gustaf Rossby. He told her about a new program that taught US military pilots about weather.

This program came at a good time. The United States had recently entered **World War II**. Joanne wanted to help the war effort. She planned to join the Navy's Women Accepted for Volunteer Emergency Service, or WAVES. But to do this, Joanne would have to leave college. Her parents did not want her to do that.

Joanne still wanted to help. So she joined the program Professor Rossby had told her about. For nine months, she trained to be a weather officer. In May 1943, she began teaching military pilots about weather. She worked at both the University of Chicago and New York University.

Joanne began her weather officer training at the University of Chicago.

HEAD IN THE CLOUDS

>> *In 1989, Simpson became the first female president of the American Meteorological Society.*

While working as a weather officer, Simpson continued her studies. She graduated in 1943. Then **World War II** ended, and so did Simpson's job.

After the war, many women returned to their roles as wives and mothers. But Simpson decided to continue her education.

Simpson stayed at the University of Chicago to study **meteorology**. In 1945, she graduated. Then, Simpson wanted to earn her **PhD**.

An adviser told Simpson women should not be meteorologists. He explained that meteorologists worked night shifts at airports. They flew in airplanes to do research. He said women could not do these things!

The adviser went on to say that no woman had ever earned a PhD in meteorology. In addition, he believed none ever would. And even if one did, she would not be able to get a job in the field! Simpson disagreed.

Simpson became known for her study of hot towers and large cumulus clouds.

NEVER SAY NEVER

Simpson refused to believe what the adviser had said. She was committed to her goals. To continue her studies, she took out student loans. She also began teaching at the Illinois Institute of Technology (IIT) in Chicago.

At IIT, Simpson met Professor Herbert Riehl. He lectured there on tropical storm research. Simpson found these storms fascinating. She asked Riehl if he would be her **PhD** adviser. He said yes!

Simpson then met with Professor Rossby at the University of Chicago. She told him about her plan to study tropical clouds. Rossby agreed to Simpson's plan. He felt that clouds were a good subject "for a little girl to study."

At the time, scientists did not think clouds were that important. They believed clouds were only a result of weather systems, not a cause of them.

In 1949, Simpson became the first American woman to earn a PhD in **meteorology**. Soon, she would begin to change the way the world thought about clouds. Simpson's research would show that clouds do indeed cause weather systems.

Simpson and her husband (center) spent time with Riehl (right).

13

WOODS HOLE

>> *A lack of ladies restrooms on airplanes was a surprisingly big obstacle to Simpson's career.*

As she had been warned, Simpson had trouble finding work in her field. For a while she taught at IIT. Then in 1951, Simpson finally found work as a **meteorologist**. Her new job was at the Woods Hole Oceanographic Institute on Cape Cod.

At Woods Hole, Simpson wanted to learn more about tropical clouds. She asked for a plane that would allow her to measure them.

The US Navy loaned Woods Hole a plane for this purpose. The scientists added special instruments for studying the clouds.

Even though the plane had been Simpson's idea, there was a problem. Woods Hole did not allow women to fly! Luckily, the officer in charge of the plane demanded Simpson be allowed to go.

Simpson took many long flights over the tropical Pacific Ocean. During these flights, she filmed clouds as they formed. Later, she drew maps based on her films. For the

first time, scientists could see patterns in the ways clouds form. Simpson created the first scientific cloud model from this information.

HOT TOWERS AND HURRICANES

>> *During its life cycle, a hurricane can give off as much energy as 10,000 nuclear bombs!*

Simpson quickly became well known. In 1954, she won a Guggenheim **Fellowship** to work in England. And in 1955, she was an honorary lecturer at London's Imperial College.

During those two years, five major hurricanes hit the eastern United States. Afterward, the US Congress asked Simpson to be an adviser on the new Hurricane Research Program.

Simpson also continued to work with Professor Riehl. In 1958, they released their "Hot Tower" **hypothesis**. Hot towers are tall clouds. They carry warm, moist air from the ocean's surface up to 50,000 feet (15,240 m) in the air. The partners claimed that these clouds move heat and moisture from the tropics to cooler areas.

Simpson also applied the hot towers idea to hurricanes. She believed the warm air was the force behind these powerful storms. Today, scientists know she was right.

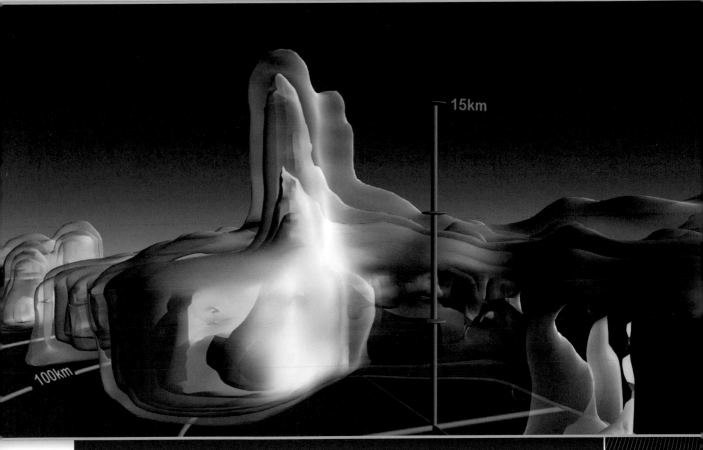

15km

100km

Hot towers form near the eye of a hurricane. Warm, moist air rises quickly inside the storm. Then, it cools and forms rain. The more rain there is, the more heat is released. This heat fuels and strengthens the storm. In 1998, Hurricane Bonnie's hot tower reached 9 miles (15 km) high!

PROJECT STORMFURY

>> *In the early 1970s, Robert Simpson helped design the Saffir-Simpson Hurricane Intensity Scale.*

In 1960, Simpson left Woods Hole to teach at the University of California–Los Angeles (UCLA). Meanwhile, she wrote two books. She also updated her cloud model with new computer calculators.

In 1964, Simpson joined the National Weather Bureau (NWB). At the NWB, Simpson met a **meteorologist** named Robert Simpson. He headed the NWB's Severe Storms Program.

Simpson had been married twice before. Both marriages had failed. But in 1965, she married Robert. Their marriage lasted for the rest of her life.

Shortly after their marriage, Robert became director of the National Hurricane Center (NHC) in Miami, Florida. Meanwhile, Simpson led the NHC's Experimental Meteorology Laboratory from 1965 to 1974.

Project Stormfury was part of this organization. From 1962 to 1966, Simpson worked on Stormfury. The project focused on how to weaken hurricanes. And, it allowed her to test her ideas on cloud seeding.

At UCLA, Simpson began to think about how to test her cloud model. This led to her work in cloud seeding.

PLANTING SEEDS

In cloud seeding, a chemical is introduced into a cloud. The chemical causes water droplets in the cloud to freeze and release energy.

Simpson believed that this energy release would cause the cloud to grow. In fact, she believed a seeded cloud would be twice as tall as an unseeded one!

To test her idea, Stormfury scientists flew high above the clouds and seeded them. The clouds behaved just as Simpson's models had said they would!

Unfortunately, seeding did not prove useful for weakening hurricanes. Still, Simpson and her team learned more about how clouds and storms act.

In 1974, Simpson felt ready for a change. So, she joined the University of Virginia (UVA) in Charlottesville. Simpson taught there for five years. In 1976, she became the first woman to be named W.W. Corcoran professor of **environmental** sciences.

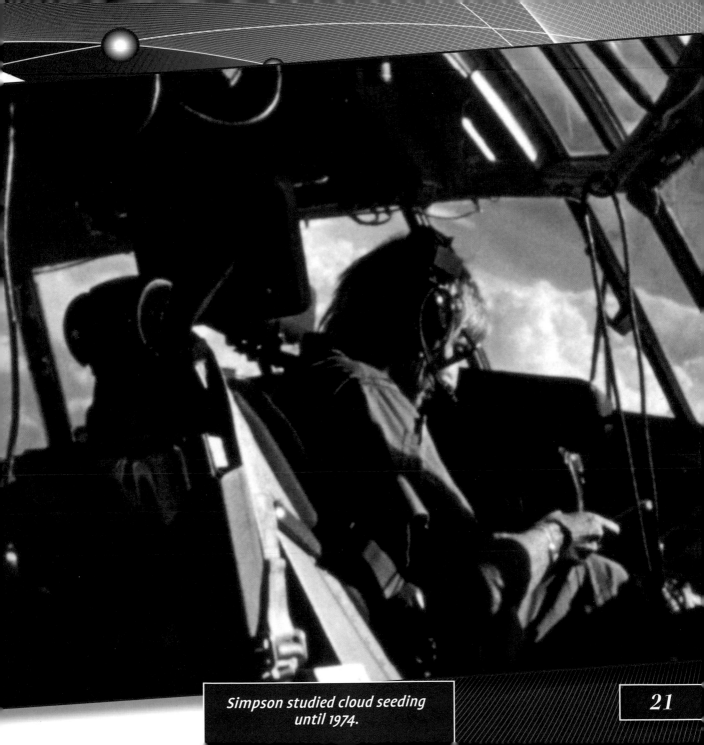

Simpson studied cloud seeding
until 1974.

AT HOME AT NASA

In 1979, the National Aeronautics and Space Administration (NASA) started the Laboratory for Atmospheres. It was at the Goddard Space Flight Center in Greenbelt, Maryland. Simpson requested a one-year leave from UVA to work at the lab.

One year off turned into two. Then in 1981, Simpson decided to stay at NASA for good. She enjoyed the female-friendly workplace. On her first visit to the restroom, she met two other women scientists!

At NASA, Simpson was in charge of the Severe Storms Board from 1979 to 1988. After that, she became chief scientist of **meteorology**.

In 1983, Simpson earned an important award. The American Meteorological Society gave her the Carl-Gustaf Rossby Research Medal. She was the first woman to win it.

In 1986, NASA asked Simpson to lead a new project. It was called the Tropical Rainfall Measuring Mission, or TRMM. TRMM was a natural fit for Simpson. She put together a team of scientists and got to work.

Simpson earned many firsts in her field. She won the Rossby medal (right). And, she was the first woman to receive the International Meteorological Organization Prize.

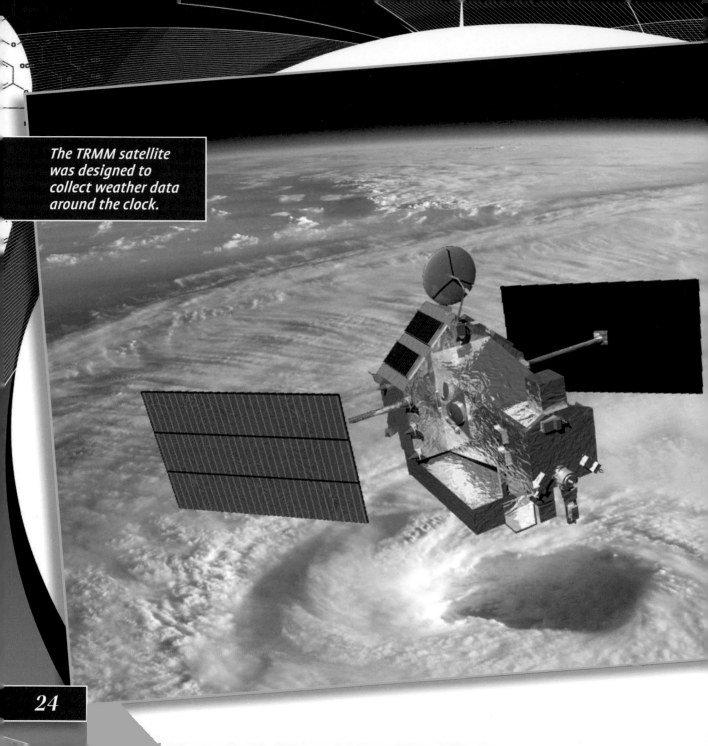

The TRMM satellite was designed to collect weather data around the clock.

The plan for TRMM was to launch a **satellite** into space. There, its **radar** would measure how much rain fell in the Earth's tropical areas.

Simpson and her team spent more than 10 years making their project a reality. Finally in 1997, they sent the first **meteorological** radar into space!

The information it gathered helped scientists learn more about tropical weather. They also learned how different climates affect each other. The radar continued to provide data for more than 15 years.

Simpson considered TRMM to be her greatest contribution to science. The project led to many weather discoveries. It showed how hurricanes form over the Atlantic Ocean. And, it revealed how dust and smoke affect rainfall.

LASTING WORDS

Simpson had always cared about the connection between weather and climate. As a government worker, she kept her personal opinions to herself. But after retiring, Simpson surprised the science community. She spoke out on **climate change**.

Simpson said more data was needed to learn the cause of climate change. She urged scientists to look beyond greenhouse gases. She believed changes in population growth and land use could also be factors.

Simpson also spoke out about the challenges of balancing motherhood and work. She raised three children without the help of day care. She had to hire babysitters or bring her children to work with her. Simpson was proud that all three chose to work in science.

Dr. Joanne Simpson loved her work. She hoped never to retire! She nearly reached that goal. She died on March 4, 2010, not long after leaving NASA. But Simpson's commitment to **meteorology** lives on. We see it every time we tune in to the local weather report.

In 2006, Simpson became a member of the American Academy of Arts and Sciences.

TIMELINE

1923	1939	1943	1949	1958	1962
On March 23, Joanne Gerould was born in Boston, Massachusetts.	At age 16, Joanne earned her pilot's license.	Simpson graduated from the University of Chicago in Illinois.	Simpson became the first woman to earn a PhD in meteorology from the University of Chicago.	Simpson and Professor Herbert Riehl released their "Hot Tower" hypothesis.	Simpson began experimenting with cloud seeding for Project Stormfury.

1976	1979	1983	1986	1997	2010
Simpson became the first woman named a W.W. Corcoran professor of environmental sciences at the University of Virginia in Charlottesville.	Simpson began working at NASA's Goddard Space Flight Center in Greenbelt, Maryland.	Simpson became the first woman to win the Carl-Gustaf Rossby Research Medal.	NASA asked Simpson to lead the Tropical Rainfall Measuring Mission (TRMM).	Simpson and her team launched TRMM into space.	On March 4, Simpson died in Washington DC.

DIG DEEPER

Many factors come into play to cause weather changes. In addition to clouds, Dr. Joanne Simpson studied rainfall, temperature change, and wind speed. Make your own anemometer to measure the power of the wind!

SUPPLIES:
• 5 small paper cups • 2 straight plastic straws • a "T" pin • a pencil with eraser • a 1-hole punch • a stapler • a marker

INSTRUCTIONS: *Always ask an adult for help!*

1 Punch a hole in four of the cups, about 0.5 inches (1.3 cm) below the rim. Use the pencil to mark the side of the cups opposite from the hole. Take the fifth cup and punch four equally spaced holes, about 0.25 inches (0.6 cm) below the rim. In the center of the bottom of the fifth cup, poke a hole with the pin. Make the hole larger with the pencil.

2 Take a straw and push it through the hole of one cup until it reaches the other side. Fold the end of the straw and staple it to the side of the cup where marked. Repeat with the second straw and a second cup.

3 Take the four-hole cup and push the open end of one straw through so the straw exits the other side. Attach a loose cup to the open end of the straw. Make sure the two cups face opposite directions. Staple in place. Repeat with the remaining two straws and cups. Make sure the open ends of all four cups go the same direction around.

4 Using the pin, secure the straws where they cross. Put the eraser end of the pencil through the hole of the center cup. Push the pin into it as far as it will go. Mark one cup with the marker. This will help you count rotations.

Take your anemometer outside for a test run. It should rotate with the wind, like a pinwheel. Observe the wind speed at various times and record your findings. The more rotations you count, the faster the wind is blowing!

GLOSSARY

aviation – the operation and navigation of aircraft. A person who operates aircraft is called an aviator.

climate change – a long-term change in Earth's climate, or in that of a region of Earth. It includes changing temperatures, weather patterns, and more. It can result from natural processes or human activities.

environment – all the surroundings that affect the growth and well-being of a living thing.

fellowship – the position of a person appointed for advanced study or research.

hypothesis (heye-PAH-thuh-suhs) – an unproven idea or theory based on known facts that leads to further study.

meteorology (mee-tee-uh-RAH-luh-jee) – a science that deals with weather and the atmosphere. Someone who works with weather is a meteorologist.

PhD – doctor of philosophy. Usually, this is the highest degree a student can earn.

radar – an instrument that uses the reflection of radio waves to detect and track objects.

satellite – a manufactured object that orbits Earth. It relays scientific information back to Earth.

World War II – from 1939 to 1945, fought in Europe, Asia, and Africa. Great Britain, France, the United States, the Soviet Union, and their allies were on one side. Germany, Italy, Japan, and their allies were on the other side.

WEB SITES

To learn more about Joanne Simpson, visit ABDO Publishing Company online. Web sites about Joanne Simpson are featured on our Book Links page. These links are routinely monitored and updated to provide the most current information available.

www.abdopublishing.com

INDEX